Folk Tales of Sherpa and Yeti

Nirala Series
FOLK TALES OF SHERPA AND YETI

Shiva Dhakal (1950-), born at Palung, Narayani Zone of Central Nepal, is a well-known short story writer, folklorist and journalist. He was educated mainly at the Tribhuvan University, A widely travelled author, Mr. Dhakal received much acclaim from Nepalese critics for his book of short-stories, entitled *Topchara ko Gunda* (An Orian's Nest and Other stories). In 1989, he published his book of travelogues entitled, *Jeevan ka Doba Haru* (Footprints of Life). *Folk Tales of Sherpa and Yeti* was written during his trek to Rolwaling and Khumbu. Mr. Dhakal is known for his penetrating essays on ecological and environmental aspects of the Nepalese landscapes. Much respectred as a literary figure in Nepal, Mr. Dhakal is busy preparing his manuscript on the lore and legend of the Kathmandu Valley.

Currently, Mr. Dhakal lives in Kathmandu and is associated with *Naya Patrika Daily*.

Recipient of fellowships and grants from The Rockefeller Foundation, Ireland Literature Exchange, The Institute for the Translation of Hebrew Literature and The Foundation for the Production and Translation of Dutch Literature, **Yuyutsu RD Sharma** is a distinguished poet and translator. He has published seven poetry collections, including, *Annapurna Poems*, (Nirala, 2008) *www.WayToEverest.de: A photographic and Poetic Journey to the Foot of Everest,* (Epsilonmedia, Germany, 2006) with German photographer Andreas Stimm and recently a translation of Irish poet Cathal O' Searcaigh poetry in Nepali in a bilingual collection entitled, *Kathmandu: Poems: Selected and New,* 2006. He has translated and edited several anthologies of contemporary Nepali poetry in English and launched a literary movement, *Kathya Kayakalpa* (Content Metamorphosis) in Nepali poetry.

Widely traveled author, he has read his works at several prestigious places including Poetry Café, London, Seamus Heaney Centre for Poetry, Belfast, Western Writers' Centre, Galway, WB Yeats' Centre, Sligo, Gustav Stressemann Institute, Bonn, Irish Writers' Centre, Dublin,

The Guardian Newsroom, London, Arnofini, Bristol, Borders, London, Royal Society of Dramatic Arts, London, Gunter Grass House, Bremen, GTZ, Kathmandu, Ruigoord, Amsterdam, Nehru Centre, London, Frankfurt Book Fair, Frankfurt, Indian International Centre, New Delhi, and Villa Serbelloni, Italy. He has held workshop in creative writing and translation at Queen's University, Belfast, and South Asian Institute, Heidelberg University, Germany.

His works have appeared in *Poetry Review, Chanrdrabhaga, Sodobnost, Amsterdam Weekly, Indian Literature, Irish Pages, Omega, Howling Dog Press, Exiled Ink, Iton77, Little Magazine, The Telegraph, Indian Express* and *Asiaweek*.

Born at Nakodar, Punjab and educated at Baring Union Christian College, Batala and later at Rajasthan University, Jaipur, Yuyutsu remained active in the literary circles of Rajasthan and acted in plays by Shakespeare, Bertolt Brecht, Harold Pinter, and Edward Albee. Later he taught at various campuses of Punjab University, and Tribhuwan University, Kathmandu.

The Library of Congress has nominated his book of Nepali translations entitled, *Roaring Recitals; Five Nepali Poets* as Best Book of the Year 2001 from Asia under the Program, *A World of Books International Perspectives*.

Yuyutsu's own work has been translated into German, French, Italian, Slovenian, Hebrew, Spanish and Dutch. He edits *Pratik*, A Magazine of Contemporary Writing and contributes literary columns to Nepal's leading daily, *The Himalayan Times* and *Newsfront Weekly*. He has completed his first novel.

More: www.yuyutsu.de

NIRALA SERIES

FOLK TALES OF SHERPA & YETI

COLLECTED BY SHIVA DHAKAL

ADAPTED FROM THE NEPALI BY
YUYUTSU RD SHARMA

Nirala

Nirala Publications
G.P.O. Box 7004
4637/20, Ground Flooor, 127,
Munish Plaza, Ansari Road,
Daryaganj, New Delhi-110002
nirlabooks@yahoo.co.in
niralapublications.com

First Edition 2017

ISBN 81-8250-084-2

Copyright @ Yuyutsu Sharma

Cover Design: Shailendra Saxena

Cover Illustration: S. Shrestha

This book is sold subject to the condition that it shall not, by way of trade or otherwise be lent, resold, hired out, or otherwise circulated without the publisher's prior written consent in any form of binding or cover other than that in which it is published and without a similar condition including this condition being imposed on the subsequent purchaser and without limiting the rights under copyright reserved, no part of this publication may be reproduced, stored in or introduced into a retrieval system or transmitted in any form or by any means (electronic, mechanical, photocopying, recording or otherwise) without prior written permission of the above mentioned publisher of this book.

Printed at
Chaman Offset, New Delhi 2

Foreword

It gives me pleasure to write the foreword to this book of folktales written by Shiva Dhaka. For systematic reading, I have divided the foreword into three parts: (A) Folklores and folk tales, (B) Sherpa people, and (C) Analysis of Shiva Dhakal's folktales. In order to make the study of folktales more scientific, I have used Henry Murray's (1938) techniques of need, press, outcome and cathexis analysis. They follow sequentially:

(I) Folklores and Folktales

'Folklore' is a translation of the German word *'Volkskunde.'* The English antiquarian William John Thoms coined the term 'folklore' in 1846. Folklore is a branch of cultural ethnology, and folktale contains oral literary tradition, which is one of the major components of folklore. Folklore symbolizes literary and artistic traditions on one hand and popular tradition on the other. It includes folk art, craft, tools, costume, folk medicine, recipes, folk-dance, games, gestures, speech, folk beliefs, legends, myths, rituals, proverbs, riddles, customs, magic, mime, deity, verse, and calendar lore.

There are folklores regarding animals, dwarfs, birds, insects, plants, fairies, diviners, witches, demons, spirits, vampires, zombies, minerals, stones, gems, stars, puns, dances, ballads, omens, festivals, ogres, and numskulls.

Apart from these, folklore is the lore of heroes, e.g. Frederick Barbarossa in Germany, the Cid in Spain, Cuchulain in Ireland, Robin Hood in England, Paul Banyan in the United States, Yu in Chain, and Prithivi Narayan Shah in Nepal.

Folklore also includes myths. Indeed, some world-famous myths are: Myths of the Greeks and Romans, e.g. Prometheus and his gift to man, Midas and the golden touch, Orpheus and Eurydice, Hercules and the golden apples. Then there are myths relating to the North American Indian; e.g. the four wishes, Blue Jay. Myths of Africa; e.g. the poor man, the sun and the children. Myths of Japan; e.g. the moon maiden, the crystal Buddha. Myth of China; e.g. the divine archer. Myths of Australia; e.g the gifts of Byamee, How the sun was made, and Myths of the Hindus; e.g. the story of Rama and Seeta, Shiva and Uma and so on. The myths of Mexico and Peru; e.g. the twin brothers.

Jonas Balys, a Lithuanian folklorist and ethnologist, asserts that folklore is the traditional creation of people, both primitive and civilized, including traditional folk-science and folk poetry. B.A.Botkin emphasizes that folklore constitutes a basic part of our oral culture. He further points to "folklore as a neglected source of social history." It throws light on man's past, and helps to reconstruct the spiritual history of man. According to Aurelio M.Espinosa, folklore reflects the mind of common, illiterate and primitive people. Jacobs and Herskovits recognize that folktales provide reference to the givers of culture, social arrangements, economic habits, linguistic structures and value systems.

In Germany, Jacob Grimm employed folklore to illuminate Germanic religion of the 'Dark Ages'. Edward Tylor, Andrew Lang and others reconstructed the beliefs and rituals of prehistoric man through their study of folklore. Marxist scholars have analyzed and asserted that folklore entirely belongs to the working-class people.

The study of folktales aims at understanding culture, society and national character or modal personality in depth. In the context of modal personality, folktales were analysed by Barnouw (1963). Like folklores, folktales also contain symbolic motifs—conscious as well as unconscious. They too contain cognitive and expressive referents and may represent characteristic patterns of society, its defense processes and reaction patterns. Folk fantasy and memory play a negative role in the constitution of prejudices, stereotypes, fales beliefs, and daydreams. Professor Stith Thompson, the folklorist has mentioned that riddles are sweeter than honey.

The legends of the Pied Piper of Hamelin or Lady Godiva, and the legends of Gargantua are famous all over the world. Folklore in the Old Testament as well as the Arabian Night, the Cupid and Psyche may be seen as sourcebook for West Asian folklore. French folktales of "Romans dela Table Rounde," "The White Cat," "Cinderela", "The Master Thief" and "Pyramus and Thisbe"are very interesting too.

In Japan, the Fox and Badger is a very famous folktale. A lot of Japanese folklore may be found in the book, *The Kojiki*. Japan is rich in fairy tales, and festival lores like 'Choya' (Chrysanthemum festival on September 9).

Oddly enough, New Yorkers celebrate September 9 as "Double Nine Day, Festival of High Places." The Chippewa of North Minnesota celebrate New Year's Day as "Kissing day" and April 1 as "All Fool's Day." The Nepalese Hindu Calendar has many festivals like Mother's Day, Father's Day, Shri Panchami, Vijaya Dashami, Deepawali, Krishna Ashtami, Teej, and Indra Jatra. Similarly, Sherpas celebrate Mani Rimdu and Losar. They also participate in 'Nyungne' rite, and act of penance for purification. Its essential elements are chorten, Mani-Walls, and the gompa. Prayers are addressed to *Pawa Cherenzi* (Avalokitesvara) and also to demons and to the 'lu', serpent deities (Furer-Haimendorf.1984).Nepalese folktales contain a blend of Tibetan and Hindu religious beliefs. The story of mysterious creature' Dhon Cholecha' and the 'story of seven sisters' are very popular. Newar folktales contain "Kichkanya"; "Lakhe and "bhut."

Among the famous folklorists of the nineteenth century were Oskar Dahnhardt in Germany, Paul Sebillot in France, S.O.Addy in England, and Y.M.Sokolov in Russia. Major twentieth century scholars in this field are Franz Boas, Richard Chase, Marie Campbell, Stith Thompson, K.Krohn, and Antti Aarne.

Folklore is an important source of religion. Himalayan folklores have been derived from the Vedas, the Puranas, the Mahabharat, and the Ramayan. These religious books represent the folk wisdom of ancient times. On making an analytical study of the mythologies of Himalayan, Greeks, Roman, German, and Irish people, it can be generalized that they show similar themes reflecting the minds of simple and primitive peoples. Thus, a kind of "polygenesis" is found in the origin of all these folklores of the world. The bird languages-motif is common among Hindu, Celtic, Slavic, European and Hebrew folktales.

Tara Dutt Gairola(1977) subdivides Himalayan folklore into seven parts: (a) Legends of ancient heroes, (b) Fairy tales, (c) Ghost and demon tales, (d) Bird and beast lore, (e) Magic tales, (f) Tales of wit and wisdom, (g) Ballads and songs.

According to Karan Sakya and Linda Griffith (1980) folktales of Himalayan regions show the impact of Tibetan culture and reflect the themes of religious, morals, and sexuality.

A few psychologists have taken interested in reviewing and analyzing folktales. McClelland has analyzed the achievement – motivation themes of folktales. Fisher (1963) has analyzed the socio-psychological themes of folklores. Colby (1966) emphasizes the functional aspect of folktales in socialization process of children. As an anthropologist, Colby demands new and improved methodology, to study folklores. The folktale as a cultural model could reveal the central values of various cultures.

Folklore has served as a political instrument, and accelerated the central notion of class-struggle in China, in Cube, and in the former Soviet Union. Teutonic mythology was used by the Nazis to propagate their idea of master race in pre-war Germany. Folklore also helps to validate social institutions and religious rituals, reinforces custom and taboo; and releases pent-up hostilities (Bas-outcom, 1954). Benedict (1935) points to the release of individuals' tension through folklore. Fisher (1936) suggests that folklore transforms the anti-social emotions of individuals into socially desirable ends. Bruner (1959) asserts that myths provide support for the development of personal identity.

Herskovits (1958) classifies folklore areas of the world into three: the old world, e.g.; Africa, Europe, and Asia, the south sea, e.g.; Polynesia, Melanesia; North and South America. Old world folklores employ a pantheon of gods, and super-natural beings. South sealore use magical fairy tales and dualistic hero—one wise and another foolish. North and South America significantly use explanatory plays, Trickster-transformer type, transformation of men into animals or vice versa, ancestor stories, myths about cataclysm, star myths, ghost and spirit tales and animal stories.

There has been an attempt to explain folktales by many theories. The great Max Muller explained and interpreted legends as linguistic corruptions; Jakob Grimm saw folklores as corrupted cosmic allegories; E. Tylor and Andrew Lang viewed them to be survivals from a savage society; and Freud considered them as sexual symbolism. None of these theories can accurately account for folklore. Hence, a combination of these theories could perhaps interpret folklore somewhat adequately.

Finnish scholar Kaarle Krohn developed the "historical-geographical method" of folklore research. Colby (1966) used computer analysis for the study of semantic field of folklore and reported that Navajo Indian folktales contain higher frequencies of the word travel. Triandis (1972) applied the antecedent-consequent method for the analysis of folklore.

(II) The Sherpa People

This book contains twelve folktales from the vicinity of Gauri-Shankar Himal, valleys of Rolwaling and Khumbu. These two places at an average altitude of 12000 feet lie in eastern Nepal. People living in these areas are known as Sherpas, and believe in Mahayan Buddhism. They speak a Tibeto-Burman language similar to Tibetan, and have 21 clan names at present. Sherpas realize that they are superior to other Bhotias and Khambas. The chief settlement areas of Sherpas are Solu, Pharak and Khumbu.

They cultivate spinach, potatoes, buck, wheat, maize, barley and garlic, and export potatoes to Tibet. Thus, potatoes play a significant role in the summer crop-economy of Sherpas. They have winter, summer and subsidiary settlements at Namche, Thami, Pangboche, Deoje,and Dingboche. Their villages and settlements contain Buddhist temple, gompa, stupa, chorten, and mani-walls. Their sacred paintings, e.g. scrolls are of many colors. They welcome traders and tourists in their own houses. Generally, tourists face no problems in 'lodging'. Their houses are either single or two storeyed. Sherpa economy depends mostly on raising and sale of cattle like Nak, Yak, Zopkiok, Zhum; also goat, sheep, lang and horse. Sherpas also depends on sale of butter and tea, which they export to Tibet. They are often employed as porters and assistants by high altitude mountaineering expeditions. Sometimes they export raw wool from Nepalese sheep and highland goat. Thus trekking, wage labor and shopkeeping form alternative vocations for Sherpas.

Lama Sange Dorje was the founder of Thami's gompa, which is very old and famous for its historic tradition. Lamas of this gompa do not observe celibacy. They marry and continue as patrons of the gompa. It is believed that Lama Sange Dorje performed miracles and ultimately died at Rongphu.

The Sherpa people, though very traditional, live in a nuclear family after marriage. The joint family system has ceased to function in this culture. This might be a factor of their peaceful conjugal life. In Sherpa community love and sex are not so frowned upon as in Hindu society. Sherpa girls are openhearted, cheerful, and soft in nature. They accept friends and like to chat freely and enjoy direct jokes and puns. Parents tend to agree with the wishes of their daughters for fixing the date of marriage. They do not exhibit 'shame' for their sexual conduct. Coition is considered a natural process bearing no stigma of guilt. They generally marry in the same village. Even giving birth to an illegitimate child is not considered disgraceful. However, unlike Gurungs, marriage among cross-cousins is prohibited. Sexual relations grow rapidly after engagement. However, sometimes, engagements may be broken owing to time and situation-constraints.

'Dem-Chang' ceremony is known as an initial wedding rite while 'Zendi' is the final wedding rite, and confirmation of marriage but the children born after 'Dem-chang' are considered legitimate and there is a shortcut wedding ceremony also known as 'Rit'. The Sherpas practice both polyandrous and polygamous marriages. Some husbands who live in the mother-in-law's house are called "maksu," resident son-in-law.

The Sherpas are devotees of Guru Rimpoche. They celebrate *Dumje* and *Narak* festivals during the Monsoon and autumn seasons respectively. They have strong faith in witches, *pem* and malignant spirits, *shrindi*. The Sherpa shaman is known as *Ihawa*, and is believed to be able to see and hear the spirits. "Tsirim" rite can free them from evil spirits. The dance-drama 'Mani- Rimdu' portrays the victory of Buddhism over the demons and is usually performed in the monastery at Thyangboche in the month of May every year.

(III) Analysis of Shiva Dhakal's Folktales

Here the themes of Dhakal's folktales are briefly explained to understand them:

(1) *Rolwaling's Gauri Shankar*

This folktale exhibits the impact of Hindu culture and religion on Sherpa People. The story is as follows: - Owing to conflict between Gauri and her husband, she leaves her house. Her elder brother-in-law (Jethaju), Shankar becomes concerned and goes out to look for her. Eventually one day they meet but are unable to talk. Gauri is ashamed and Shankar surprised. The essence of the tale is that the family relation can be continued only with love, affection, and concern. A sublime love for one's brother and sister-in-law is shown in this tale. It reflects the needs of autonomy, rejection, dominance, play, aggression, and deference.

(2) Annihilation of the Yeti

How Sherpas get rid of the trouble caused by Yeti, is the theme of this tale. Brave Sherpas enact a drama to present artificial fighting and drinking 'Chyang' a local wine. Yetis imitate the situation unconsciously and actually fight each other and die. It is a tale of unconscious imitation. Very few Yetis survive this incident. This tale brings out the jealousy of Yetis with the Sherpa people. A scene of "Chhyang-Psychosis" among Yetis is interesting. The moral of this tale is that blind imitation is always dangerous. It shows the needs of aggression, and constrain, and press of autonomy and coercion.

(3) Tit for Tat

The story moves around two cultural settings. This tale delineates the character of crooked friends and their simple wives. Its theme is the infidelity of two friends belonging to different castes, Newar and Sherpa. This exposes the illicit sexual relationships between the character and his friend's wife. Both friends, Dharma Ratan and Mingma Norbu show insatiable sex urges. Coition is metaphorized by locking and unlocking the 'padlock', which signifies the structure of Vagina. It is really a Freudian View. The essence of this tale is 'Sex-revenge'. Its moral is that one must not be faithless to an intimate friend. In other words, disloyalty begets disbelief. The tale centers on the *Somar* and *Chhyang* drink-culture of Sherpas. Interpreted according to the Freudian view, Dharma Ratan and Mingma Norbu's superegos are not developed. Their wives' superegos were weak and devoid of guilt feelings. This tale expresses the needs of sex, aggression, and sentience, and the press of heterosexual seduction.

(4) Flying Deerskin

This tale shows the impact of Hindu Culture on Sherpas. The hero of this tale is Kalwar who belongs to Hindu stock. It is a fantastic, magical tale of infidelity and bravery of the Kalwar whom the king offers his daughter. Later Kalwar brings down the dwarf, 'One-footer man' and puts him to the sword. The two wrestler friends of Kalwar take away a woman. The blind old uncle rewards Kalwar with stick, rope, and deerskin as he brings back his eyes from the devil. Kalwar avenges himself on his fraudulent friends who had stolen away a young woman and goes back to the palace; later he defeats the king and reigns peacefully with the Princess, now his queen. The moral of the tale is that a brave man can accomplish many heroic deeds. It shows the need of aggression, dominance and achievement.

(5) Sonam and Yeti in Chhringma's Lap

In this folktale, the quiet-looking Sonam goes out to bring three pieces of leafy pine stems for the 'name-giving' ceremony of his son. He sees hairy 'one-footer-man', a disguised Yeti, who can transform his body into Chhui-Mui and 'Chhelma'. Sonam has heard that 'Chhelma' has been a man-eater. Yeti's height increases as the sun comes up. Sonam is shocked and loses his consciousness, as he sees Yeti. The Lama takes care of him for months till he recovers. There is a Sherpa folk-belief that if a man happens to see a Yeti, he loses his awareness and energy. This tale reflects the press of physical danger and strain with misfortune.

(6) Harital

In this tale, the orphan Gyaljen joins his wife as a resident son-in-law, Maksu, after his marriage. His mother-in-law lives with them. Gyaljen is under psychological pressure, and suffers from inferiority complex .Most of the time he is insulted by his wife and mother-in-law. She (mother-in-low) is an expert in 'Harital' black magic and practices it to cheat rich tourists. Gyaljen, however, is very unaware of this trick. Their home is like a pub that these guests and tourists visit and there the old magician cheats them. Gyaljen is innocent and he being afraid of the situation suddenly leaves the home. Life is like a business to Gyaljen's wife and mother-in-law. It is all a misfortune for Gyaljen. This tale contains poverty and rejection press, and exhibition, inavoidance, and rejection needs also.

(7) Sange Dorje's Gompa in the Lap of Amadablan

This mythical tale centers on the saintly Sange Dorje Lama of 'Rongfu Gompa'. This gompa was situated to the north of Everest, *Chhomolongma*. He traveled to Pangboche from Rongfu. After he shaves his face, many pine plants grow out of his beard. The spot where Sange Dorje had meditated now becomes a place of pilgrimage. Thus, he is regarded as an incarnate Lama. Amadablam is seen as an ornament of nature, where Sange Dorje was revered by all the peoples of Khumbu. This story expresses the needs of understanding and order.

(8) The Ravishing of Angnima by a Yeti

In this tale, a Yeti rapes Angnima, a shy Sherpa virgin girl of twenty-one. Like a man-eater, Yeti destroys her. Angnima's health gradually runs down after the rape incident, and she ultimately dies within a month. This tale exposes the dangers posed by Yeti and seduction press.

(9) Snow-slide on Dorje Salt

This tale highlights the unpredictable and challenging mountain ecology of Nepal, where life is very difficult. It is a tale of two Sherpas, who are busy traveling in course of their salt and herb trade and are trapped by a 'virgin-ghost'. The Sherpas are staying in Beding village of Rolwaling. Nothing can be done to ease the difficult nature of mountain-life. He has ten'Zopkioks and during the business tour, a 'virgin-ghost' troubles him. She traps him and forces him to have coitus with her. Ultimately, she promises not to trouble travelers. On his way back, the hero faces the danger of dampness. The whole load of salt melts into water, and all the Zopkioks are frozen to death. The hero of this tale suffers from poverty, seduction, and disaster.

(10) Chhiringma's Judgment

This tale is based on the conflict between two natural forces, wind and fog. During the duel, fog gets diffused, and slowly covers the valley and peaks. The wind is furious but is unable to uproot even the small coniferous plants. When it is all over, both the parties present themselves before, Jomo Chhiringma for judgment. She announces the victory of fog and defeat of wind. Wind is disappointed and returns. Similarly, fog too goes back. The proud wind troubles the people and is hated by all, where as fog is loved by all owing to his humble nature. Pride always fails where as humility always wins. This tale expresses the needs of aggression and rejection.

In the analysis of folktales, certain dimensions are useful, e.g.; reference, function, cathexis, outcome, need, and press, for cross-cultural comparisons.

Dhakal's folktales reveal philosophy and ethics (29.16%), human behavior (25%), and nature (20.83%) according to priority of reference. Some fields expressed more than two references even (see Table 1). These folktales serve to establish ideals (36.36%), or of giving warning (27.27%), they also give information and encouragement (See Table 6). Positive Cathexis (54.54%) occurs more often than the negative

(45.45%). Some folktales reveal more than one Cathexis. The outcome is 100% definite in all these folktales. It is real (90%) and 10% was unreal but only 69% folktales have a happy outcome (see Tables 3 & 4). The intensity of need of aggression ranks first. Then come the need of sex and rejection (see Table 5). The press of 'heterosexual seduction' and 'misfortune' rank highest. One tale expresses the press of 'Yeti danger' that is a unique feature of Sherpa Culture.

Table 1
Field of Reference in Folktales

Field	Frequency	Percent
(1) Philosophy and Ethics	7	29.16
(2) Human Behavior	6	25
(3) Nature	5	20.83
(4) Animal Behavior	3	12.5
(5) Occupations	2	8.33
(6) Domesticity	1	4.16
Total 24 100 (Approx)		

* Some fields show more than two references so the total exceeds more than ten.

Table 2
Press in Folktales

Press	Frequency	Rank
1. Autonomy	2	4.5
2. Aggression	1	12
3. Coercion	2	4.5
4. Danger (Physical)	2	4.5
5. Danger (Yeti)	1	12
6. Danger (Snow & Water)	1	12
7. Death of Parents	1	12
8. Deception	1	12
9. Family discord	1	12
10. Heterosexual Seduction	3	1.5

11. Misfortune	3	1.5
12. Physical Strain	1	12
13. Poverty	2	4.5
14. Praise	1	12
15. Rejection	1	12
16. Religious training	1	12
17. Weather	1	12

Table 3
Cathexis in Folktales

Cathexis	Frequency	Percent
Positive	6	54.54
Negative	5	45.45
Total	11	100

* Some folktales reveal more than one Cathexis.

Table 4
Outcome in Folktales

Outcome	Frequency	Total	Percent	Total
Definite	10		100	
		10		100
Indefinite	0		0	
Real	9		90	
		10		100
Unreal	1		10	
Happy	6		60	
		10		100
Unhappy	4		40	

Table 5
Needs in Folktales

Need	Frequency	Rank
(1) Aggression	5	1
(2) Autonomy	1	11
(3) Achievement	1	11
(4) Contrarian	1	11
(5) Dependence	1	11
(6) Deference	1	11
(7) Dominance	2	4.5
(8) Exhibition	1	11
(9) Harm avoidance	1	11
(10) In avoidance	1	11
(11) Order	1	11
(12) Play	1	11
(13) Rejection	3	2.5
(14) Sentience	2	4.5
(15) Sex	3	2.5
(16) Understanding	1	11

Table 6
Factions of Folktales

*Function	Frequency	Percent
(1) Establishing Ideal	4	36.36
(2) Giving Warning	3	27.27
(3) Giving Information	1	9.09
(4) Giving Encouragement	1	9.09
(5) Forbidding	1	9.09
(6) Reconciling	1	9.09
Total	11	100

* Some folktales contain more than one function.

The analysis of these folktales is utilized for understanding Sherpa character. It also helps in the delineation of the model personality of Sherpas. These folktales predominantly express the needs of aggression, rejection, sex, dominance, and sentience.

As a collector of these folktales, Dhakal's efforts are praise worthy. He personally took field trips to Rolwaling and Khumbu and stayed in the area for nearly six months. He is a well-known essayist and a storywriter also. This book is an excellent contribution to Sherpa Culture and Ethnology. Dhakal deserves congratulations on his arduous undertaking involving mountain trekking and his successful recapitulation of these tales in a very simple and clear-cut style. His open and thoughtful nature attracts everyone.

-**Murari Prasad Regmi**

Preface

"Be it folk literature or culture, it contains life's unwritten history. Folk tale is a creative medium of comprehending a nation's age long value system and traditions. Of course, one might find a rich display of entertainment, and even light subjects in a folk tale. But that wouldn't mean that a folk tale is nothing but a cheap time passing tool of recreation. Man possesses a turbulent heart. He possesses oceans of feeling. He possesses a special sensibility which enables him to face innumerable attacks and counter-attacks for the sake of survival. Folk tales depict a vibrant spectrum of such evocation, moves, and counter-moves which later make history." In this context, Nepalese folktales depict uncountable pangs of agony that long settled traditional value-system cursed Nepalese masses to endure.

Folk Tales of Sherpa and Yeti does not contain tales of luxuriant drawing rooms of the Kathmandu valley. They try to capture the fire of the struggling human being. The journey of the human beings here is the journey of the history of Himal which can't be described in this brief thanks giving note.

The Beding village of Rolwaling snow-ranges is the paraxial landscape that I can never forget in my life. To the south of Gauri Shankar Himal at the height of about thirteen thousand feet lay Base camp where I spent one and a half month of my brief trek. Descending down Dholka and passing along the banks of river Tamakosi, I encountered several villages like Pekhuti, Bhorle, Suridobhan, Jagat, Seemigoon and Kialche. Along with these villages, Gauri Shanker Base camp and the Beding village became the basic backdrop of these tales. My second journey to Himal was the result of Khumbu valley. My movement from Namche Bazar to Dingboche village of Amadablam Himal marks the second area of my journey.

Sardar Passang Noubu Sherpa (Namche), Ngwang Sherpa and his old father "Pala" (Beding) Gopal Tamang and Padam Gurung emerged like angelic figures as I sat to recreate the tales. Same can also be said of Angjambu Sherpa and his father (Pangbuche) Rinchen Karma (Fakding), an about 20 year old Sange Nawa (The Protector of the Forest) who too helped me a great deal in knowing the inner drama of Sherpa mind.

I am highly grateful to Dr. Murari P. Regmi for writing a systematic analysis of the tales.

Without the help of Mrs.Mana Dhakal I cound't have reached the heights of Beding and Khumbu. I am indebted to her for her inspiration.

Finally, I thank Nirala Publications for bringing my work to light.

- **Shiva Dhakal**

Contents

Foreword — vii

Preface — xxiii

Folk Tales

Chapter One
A Lama's Sin — 1

Chapter Two
Rolwaling's Gauri Shankar — 9

Chapter Three
Annihilation of the Yeti — 15

Chapter Four
Chhiringma's Judgment — 23

Chapter Five
Flying Deerskin — 31

Chapter Six
Harital — 43

Chapter Seven
Sange Dorjee's Gompa in the Lap of Amadablam — 51

Chapter Eight   57
Snow Slide on Dorje's Salt

Chapter Nine   67
The Ravishing of Angnima by a Yeti

Chapter Ten   75
Tit for Tat

Chapter Eleven   83
Yeti's Cave

Folk Tales of Sherpa and Yeti

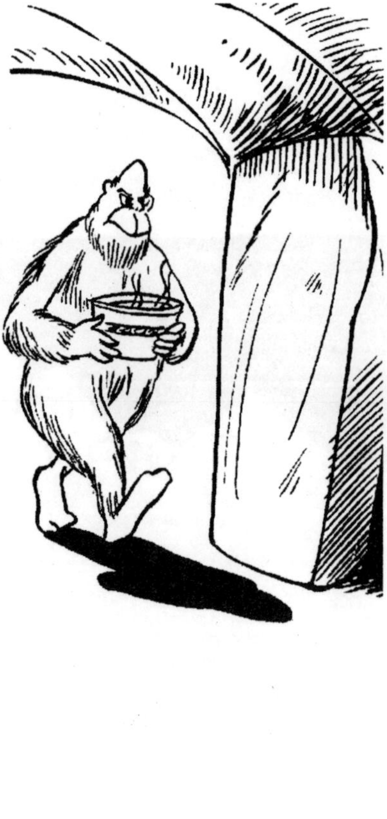

A Lama's Sin

Once there was a gompa in the village of Rolwaling. A renowned incarnate Lama used to live and lead the life of an ascetic there. Since everyone in the gompa revered him and fed him without letting him do any physical work, the incarnate enjoyed a distinct, enviable position.

Watching the plump and charming butter-like body of this young Lama, the young Sherpa girls had no choice but to moan and swallow their lusts down their throats with hot, simmering sighs.

As the custom, it was not appropriate for a Lama to exchange amorous glances with young single girls. Yet all the time a fear lurked in the hearts of the elderly members of the gompa. If young boys and girls did not exchange the imperative glances, wouldn't the entire process of creation come to an end?

While the number of the lama-thawas surpassed the ordinary householders, it was neither profane nor unholy but inevitable natural instinct between a male and a female. Yet, the elderly members favored a strict watch, fearing there might develop an affair between a Lama-thawas and a local daughter.

Chhringphuti of Beding was a Sherpa maiden of illustrious beauty. She not only possessed a lush provocative body but a shrewd mind. Infatuated by the Lama, she cooked up a plan to hook him.

"What pleasure would it be to make love to a Lama who is not only attractive and incarnate but untouched by any female presence," Chhringphuti thought and resolved to make Lama her own for the rest of her life. Dreaming thus, she dozed off into a deep slumber.

Next morning as the bigul and drum beatings of the gompa shook her sweet sleep. Chhringphuti got up and geared like a female warrior. All set to win a war.

Carrying a stout little lamb and a tipli full of *chyang*, she marched to the gompa.

The thawas of the gompa had gone away to perform their daily duties and the devotees had gone back to their respective homes. The incarnate Lama sat, lazily dozing there.

On finding a dazzling young girl with a tipli of local wine and a young lamb, the Lama incarnate was overjoyed.

Offering a tipli of beer and lamb at the Lama's holy feet, Chhiringphuti smiled and made a special request to the Incarnate, "Would Your Holiness taste the offering to bless a devotee who has brought it so painstakingly in your service."

It was not in Lama's religion to taste the wine and a lamb's meat. Then a refusal to a young devotee would just as well annoy the God.

The Lama found himself trapped in a predicament. Within seconds, he found himself tottering on a delicate thread.

"Would Your Holiness taste the offering to bless a devotee who has brought it so painstakingly in your service."

More he looked at the lustrous devotee, harder it became for him to decline her special request. Having accepted one glass of the *chyang*, he couldn't stop pouring many more down his throat.

While the *chyang* started working on the robust lama, the odor of the soft lamb's meat started tickling the incarnate conscience. On receiving the order of hacking the lamb, Chhringphuti too became ecstatic.

Now the *chyang* and soft lamb's meat became a blessed food for the holy man. That's what Chhiringphuti had wanted with all her heart.

Having taken a large amount of *chyang*, the lama started throwing impious glances at Chhiringphuti. Then there came a moment when both of them got entangled, and soon after became one.

That day Chhiringphuti's operation became successful. Nevertheless, there came an unprecidented earthquake in the gompa.

The thing that happened between Lama and Chhiringphuti shook the entire village too. The villagers punished the Lama who could not manage to remain within the limits of an incarnate's celibacy.

He had to leave the village to settle at a place named, *Na*, near Dudhkund. Chhiringphuti too was with him.

However, there was not a single visitor from Beding to reach them at that cold and remote *Na*.

The villagers punished the Lama who could not manage to remain within the limits of an incarnate's celibacy.

Rolwaling's Gauri Shankar

It is an event of bygone days. Shankar's family used to live happily in Rolwaling. Shankar had a younger brother. Gauri was his sister-in-law.

Shankar himself had not married for some unknown reasons. Everyone in the village swore of their goodwill and amicability. Shankar lived happily with his brother and sister-in-law. It was a well-knit family.

One day between Shankar's brother and his wife a bitter quarrel took place. The sister-in law, Gauri, flew into a fit of rage and left Shankar's brother and his house.

That very day Shankar was not at home. Having gathered fruits and wildflowers in the jungle, he returned late in the evening. On seeing his gloomy brother and not his favorite sister-in law, Shankar felt sick within. A fatal wave of chill crept though his heart.

At first, his brother hesitated to tell him anything about the quarrel. Since he had lied to Shankar, he narrated the details of what happened. However, where she might have gone, even the brother had no idea.

On seeing his well-knit family falling apart in a fraction of a second, Shankar became very disappointed.

At first, his brother hesitated to tell him
anything about the quarrel.

He immediately set out to search for his sister-in-law. He searched each and every corner of the hillside. But Gauri was nowhere to be found.

By the end of the day, Shanker did not feel like returning home without his goddess like sister-in-law.

One day, the sun flashed profusely and the valley grew warm. Under the shade of a juniper tree, Shanker was lying drowsy. After a while cries of an imperial pheasant disturbed his sleep.

He looked across the meadow and there in the distance come in his view a young woman frolicking with a young stag. She looked like his lost sister-in-law. Could she be Gauri?

Surely, this is his Gauri. Shankar got up and moved passionately towards the valley.

Shankar from this end began to climb while Gauri on the other was descending, playing with a young lamb.

Abruptly, both confronted each other. Yes, this is his sister in-law! Yes, here is our Gauri!

Since the sister-in- law should never ever face the elder brother-in-law barefaced, Gauri instantly flung her shawl over her face.

Then and there, both froze and became rocks.

The shawl of snow that Gauri had flung over her head did not ever break and on the top of Shankar's head snow never came to dwell.

Then and there, both froze and became rocks.

Annihilation of the Yeti

It happened long ago. Yetis used to torment the villagers a great deal. As the violence became intolerable, the elders of the village gathered and chartered a plan to get rid of this Yeti menace.

The plan they made was to bring about the Yetis into drinking *chyang*, the local millet or rice beer. Then when the time was ripe, these creatures were to be completely eradicated.

Everyone agreed and nodded ardently, for all were keen to get ride of this nuisance.

Next day, the villagers gathered at the high alpine pasture and everyone brought a large kettle of *chyang*. They had also carried with them sticks and weapons like swords and knives to carry out the operation

They stayed there and enjoyed themselves the whole day drinking and laughing, singing and dancing.

Once the *chyang* began to have an effect on their minds, they began to fight and beat each other with the sticks and weapons they had brought with them.

However, no one died in this fight because to tell the truth the humans were actually not fighting. They were only feigning to deceive the Yetis and as the result, no one was injured in this mock battle.

Towards evening, the villagers left for the village,

leaving behind quite a large quantity of *chyang* and the weapons at the pasture.

The villagers knew whatever they did throughout the Yetis, hidden in the mountainous terrain all around the day, had watched them attentively.

Actually, the Yetis had immensely enjoyed watching the villagers singing and dancing, drinking and fighting. They too had a mind to do something similar.

Once the villagers departed, the Yetis left their hiding place in groups and moved down to the pasture where right away they began drinking the contents in the kettles.

After a short while, most of them were tipsy enough to be violent.

They were fighting just as the villagers had done some time ago. In due course, they picked up the sticks and weapons lying nearby and started attacking each other.

In next to no time, there were dead bodies lying around everywhere in that hushed pasture. The less inebriated Yetis apprehended the danger they were in. Therefore, they opted out of this chaos and escaped, barely saving the species from extinction.

The few that escaped became extremely irate with the humans for tricking them into a death trap. At this point, these Yetis swore to take revenge.

However, they were able to do nothing as most of the population was devastated during this incident.

Hence, the remaining Yetis could do nothing but fume in frenzy. Marginalized, they began to live in caves high up in the mountains where humans could not reach.

Yetis used to torment the villagers a great deal.

From that day, they started considering human beings as their adversary. Even though their menace vanished, the species stayed behind.

That's why the Yetis appear repeatedly to torture human beings even today.

The remaining Yetis could do nothing but fume in frenzy.

Chhiringma's Judgment

Prior to the existence of man, the great Creator came along ploughing the earth. He had a plan in mind to set up a village somewhere in the lap of the remote Himalayas.

No human being could have managed to survive and settle in such a cold place. Thus, he came ploughing and reached the place called *Na*.

As darkness began to dictate daylight, he had to stop at one point. He found it hard to continue to plough during the late hours of darkness. The creator gave up and stopped his entire work for the day right there.

They say that the furrows made by the plough created the mountains in the area. These days the place is known as Rolwaling.

At the time of creation of the mountains, the wind and the Mist were also present there. Though both enjoyed Creator's favors, there developed a fierce hostility between Wind and the Mist over the passage of time.

Over and over again, they quarreled to prove their respective superiority and finally both became avowed enemies.

The Wind grew more proud and began to wreak havoc on the freshly set up human habitation by yanking the roofs off and carrying them away to a great distances.

She also troubled the trees, never permitting them to wear green foliage. She would blow fiercely and strip them bare mercilessly.

The villagers found it very difficult to survive the onslaught of spiteful Wind. Finally, they formed a delegation and marched to the Goddess *Chhiringma.*

To complain against callous terrorism of the Wind.

When *Chhiringma* heard the woes of the village delegation, she decided to judge the strength of the Wind against the Mist.

"Only after the contest," she said, "I will announce the final authority of either of the two, once and far all."

The Mist and the Wind were also present. The villagers were in favor of the Mist and so they were glad to know that the Mist would take part in the contest.

The villagers favored the Mist because once it covered the region with its white cap, a mild rain fell followed by white wool like snowflakes.

This was also the time when the Yeti attacked the village, and this was the only grudge the villagers against the Mist. However, during this period, the Wind did not have a chance to blow and everyone experienced a warm feeling.

The contestants were poised to begin and *Chhiringma* ready to judge. The wind began to boast and the Mist began to retaliate with similar jeering. Nevertheless, Chhiringma was impervious and indifferent.

Instead, she remarked, "Whichever of you is capable of covering the hills, mountains, valleys, nooks and crannies, cracks and crevices will be judged

Folk Tales of Sherpa and Yeti 27

On seeing this, the wind felt much upset and tried to smash and tear up everything into pieces with his violent force.

the one with the greater strength. Now depart and exhibit your strength so that I am able to judge fairly."

The Wind and the Mist left the gathering. Soon everyone could feel the wind's strength. He spread his wings and begun to rush off in all directions of the compass. The Mist, on the other hand, started to spread slowly.

As the hills and mountains obstructed the Wind's speed, the Mist crept over everything surely.

On seeing this, the wind felt much upset and tried to smash and tear up everything into pieces with his violent force.

Though it tried to race over at the roofs of the houses and the old trees, it was unable to bend the young pine and deodar trees on the hill slopes.

But the power to split the hills apart was not within the muscle of the arrogant and fuming wind.

When the contest was over, the weary contestants once again stood before Goddess to know final outcome.

Chhiringma sat down to pass her judgment. She right away judged the Mist better of the two. Mist was able to spread everywhere and cover everything. Wind could not even cross a small hill. In addition, his speed died away after a while.

On hearing the verdict, the Wind was angry and felt mortified. He said painfully, "Well, if I did not exist, no one would exist."

You lost this contest of strength and found out
that to be proud is improper.

Yet, *Chhringma* consoled him: "That's what you have promised to do in the form of air for all living beings. Here only your strength and pride were under test. You lost this contest of strength and found out that to be proud is improper. So go your own way and perform your duties and be the breath of all living beings."

The wind left, smarting from the blows of defeat. Even today, at times he blows ferociously to shake everything to articulate his annoyance. Everyone in Rolwaling was angry at the Wind. But they started loving the Mist more and more.

Flying Deerskin

Many years ago there lived in a village a man named Kalwar. Though he looked like simpleton, he possessed master skills of an extraordinary wrestler.

In his locality, he had crushed pride of many a brash wrestlers. Like jungle fire, Kalwar's fame as a wrestler spread in the kingdom and quickly reached the gates of the palace.

The king was perturbed to hear of Kalwar's bravery and strength. He had become used to seeing no one but his own court wrestlers on the top.

His courtiers too nourished similar delusions. Anyone outside the palace's flattery circles had to risk his life to prove his talent and strength.

On hearing the exploits of Kalwar's bravery, the king summoned his wrestlers and scolded them badly.

Overfed with eighty-four delicious dishes and nourished like son–in–laws, the court wrestlers had very little chance to win. Whatever the outcome of the contest, harshly insulted by the king's reprimand, the court wrestlers decided to face Kalwar.

To fetch Kalwar, the royal soldiers were rushed to his village. On finding the king's troops march towards his house, Kalwar shook with fear.

He was very well aware of the consequences of their arrival. People around him too became apprehensive because King's officers and soldiers had repeatedly come to torture them.

But on learning that the troops had come to take Kalwar to palace, everyone felt reassured. Kalwar too felt flattered to know that the king had called him to the palace to test his skills in wrestling. In addition, the fact that the king had summoned him to challenge his wrestlers was soothing one for him.

Saying farewell to his family and village folks, Kalwar left for the palace.

To lose the wrestling bout would certainly mean death. Kalwar knew that the king had the power to reward life or pronounce death sentence on anyone in the kingdom. His orders could turn any of his subjects in to a slave to build palaces, pools, and gardens for a lifetime. If infuriated, he may himself take out his sword and chop the head of the person he did not like.

Even though the king was considered benevolent, Kalwar's family grew depressed. A scepter of uncertainty hung over their heads.

Before Kalwar could reach the palace, he met court wrestlers. After being scolded by the king, they too were hastily heading towards Kalwar's house.

If Kalwar succeeded in defeating the court wrestlers, Kalwar was to marry the king's daughter. The king had himself made this announcement early in the morning.

Then and there, a fierce wrestling took place between Kalwar and court wrestlers. After an hour's struggle, the overfed court wrestlers lost the game.

A fierce wrestling took place between Kalwar
and court wrestlers.

Scared of the possibility of being punished by the king, the court wrestlers, with the help of the troops conspired against Kalwar, they misinformed the king about their shameless defeat.

But the other section of courtiers, who were highly annoyed with these idle and loudmouthed wrestlers, correctly brought out the fact that court wrestlers did not succeed in defeating Kalwar.

Before the King could pronounce the death sentence, he instantly dismissed them from the palace.

In order to remain true to his announcement, the king had to marry his youngest daughter to Kalwar.

Having married the princess, Kalwar left her with the king and set out for a journey for a short time. On the way, he met the court wrestlers, just dismissed from the palace.

Kalwar, was carrying a lush-green juniper tree on his head and walked under the same tree. Whenever he felt heat he climbed up the tree and sat on one of its branches and the tree began to walk by itself.

Surprised to see the charisma of Kalwar's power, the wrestlers too befriended Kalwar and joined him.

First night they lodged in the heart of a dense jungle. It wasn't possible for the rays of sunlight to enter that place. The night was cold and the place muddy. Some festering stench strangled human mind there. But there wasn't a way out as it was dark.

Anyway, they started to get things ready for dinner. Suddenly Kalwar noticed a line of fiery torches marching towards them.

Whenever he felt heat he climbed up the tree and sat on one of its branches and the tree began to walk by itself.

At first, they were frightened but on finding out that those torches were human beings, Kalwar and his friends heaved a sigh of relief. These jungle folks had not mastered the art of agriculture.

Kalwar was busy cooking. One of his friends had gone to fetch some water. The other one had gone to gather firewood. The one who had gone to get water returned with a young girl.

She was one of those jungle folks. As she had come to the brook to get water, this friend of Kalwar had grabbed her and brought her to the spot forcibly. Kalwar raised his voice against his friend's evil act but newly made friend wasn't ready to listen to him. He also declared his desire to take that girl for his wife.

Next morning Kalwar and his friend left that place. If the girl's parents came to know of this matter, it would prove dangerous to Kalwar's reputation.

Hastily they climbed up the tree and escaped without any obstruction. They did not find it hard because the tree could walk faster than human beings. As the night fell, they camped near a water well. Now they did not have to search water.

One of the friends stayed back to cook while Kalwar and the other set out to hunt. The former friend went to the well to fetch water. He lit fire and started cooking.

As he was busy cooking, a dwarf came out of the well and started beating him. The dwarf returned to the well with the pot full of half-cooked rice.

After some time, Kalwar and his friend returned from the hunt. They were feeling weary and very hungry. They got highly irritated when they

He took his Undenkhatola and flew towards the palace.

found their friend sitting dolefully with his forehead pressed between his knees. When they learnt of the mysterious dwarf, they were taken aback.

Kalwar immediately took a rope and tied it around his waist. He handed its other end to his friend and leaped into the well.

At the bottom of the well, a gray-haired old man was sleeping. Though the old man was not in a position to see, he was actually aware of what was going on around him. He came to know of Kalwar's presence and scolded, "Who the hell could it be to break in here at this hour to disturb my peace"?

"Uncle, it's me. Your nephew has come to cure you." Kalwar replied. He did something strange to that old man's eyes. The old man was able to see then!

The truth remained that long ago the dwarf had caught this old man and taken him to the water well. There he had plastered his eyes with deerskin. As Kalwar took off the deerskin, the old man began to see perfectly.

The old man was relieved and in return offered Kalwar an Udenkhatola made of deer's skin, a stick, and a rope. If Kalwar said, "Tie!" the rope would tie and if he said, "Beat" the stick would beat. It became easy for Kalwar to punish his enemies. If he wanted to fly, he would order his flying Udenkhatola to fly and that was all.

When the dwarf came back, he was furious with Kalwar. But he couldn't do anything as the old man's gifts to Kalwar had rendered the dwarf powerless. These miraculous things belonged to Kalwar now. The dwarf was badly beaten by Kalwar. He also freed the old man from the well.

Coming out of the well, Kalwar found his friends had deserted him. He took his Undenkhatola and flew towards the palace. On the way he found his friends sitting gossiping beneath a tree. He took his revenge with the help of the stick and rope.

On reaching the palace, he ordered his stick and rope to tie and beat the king. The rope and the stick justly obeyed. Thus, he became the king of that country and lived with his wife, the princess, happily ever after.

Harital

Many years ago there lived in Namche Bazar a Sherpa named Gyaljen.

Gyaljen's father had died long ago. In spite of the fact of being the only son of his parents, he didn't possess a thing in name of inherited property.

Gyaljen's father used to work with Tibetan merchants. That's why Gyaljen, barely able to satisfy the hunger of his belly, hadn't earned even a *yak* for himself. Yet Gyaljen survived, grew up, and turned into a handsome young man.

One day there came a proposal of marriage for him. Though the idea of being a *Ghar Jawai*, the son-in-law in-residence, appeared awkward and embarrassing, he accepted the proposal. He had to marry after all, and here was this rich girl ready to belong to him. Wasn't it an honor in itself?

Gyaljen was an innocent man. He didn't realize in order to avail the amenities of other's wealth, one has to put one's self-respect at stake. That's why the requirement of noble qualities in a wife didn't anyhow seem important to him. Gyaljen was more excited at the prospects of getting wealthy in-laws.

Even though for a while his conjugal life remained merry, it didn't continue to be so for long. By and by, his relationship with his wife became that of a servant and a master.

Gyaljen had to go to the jungle to collect firewood. Every morning and evening, he had to fetch water from the brook. In addition, it was his duty to assist his wife and mother-in-law in every household chore. His wife and the mother-in-law never uttered a word of praise for his efforts wholeheartedly.

Gyaljen's mother-in-law was expert in business transactions. She had also trained her daughter, teaching her all the tricks of the trade. Since their house was situated on the salt route that went towards Tibet through Khumbu, their Bhatti joint ran lucratively.

They were expert in enticing travelers. That's why their lodge was always full. They also received ample praise from the guests.

Though Gyaljen's wife and mother-in-law enjoyed good business, their neighbors considered them vicious witches adept in *Harital*, the art of poisoning through Black Magic. That's why people around didn't have good relations with them. Even Gyaljen had started feeling upset at their cagey activities.

Moreover, his wife and mother-in-law too, on their part, started dominating him. They would always abuse him for being an indolent man, enjoying life at the expense of his hardworking wife and mother-in-law. If Gyaljen dared to retort, they would threaten him to finish him off with *Harital*.

At last, Gyaljen stopped bothering about what they would do during nights. He would hear squeaking noises at other times. His wife had told him that

Folk Tales of Sherpa and Yeti

By and by, his relationship with his wife became that of a servant and a master.

squeaking noise *Che-Che* is the sound of the Black Magic, *Harital*.

He had also heard from the neighbors that this squeaking meant *Harital* and it could suck a man's blood and finally kill him. They also told him that *Harital* involves a process of pulling good luck from the wealthy guest and consequently transferring his property to someone else. On hearing all this, Gyaljen stopped sleeping during the night.

One night when Gyaljen was trying to sleep, he heard a squeaking noise and rose from his sleep with a squeal. From the other room came sounds of someone muttering strange words. It wasn't difficult to know what was happening in the other room for there were cracks in the wooden planks that separated the rooms.

As Gyaljen peeped through a crack, he saw that a young man, probably a guest, was sipping local beer.

Gyaljen's wife and his mother-in-law were talking of exercising *Harital* to ruin that young man's fortune in their own dialect. They were plotting to transfer his fortune by offering poison to him. Both the women were in half-naked state.

On seeing this, Gyaljen's heart started revolting. He couldn't bear it any more. He didn't feel like watching unjust scene. Straight away, he came out of the house.

It was midnight. Everything around was quiet. Only Dhukosi river's droning whistle could be heard.

Gyaljen instantly made a resolution. "One day I would earn power and energy to conquer *Harital*, and for sure return to finish them."

In the dead of the night, he came out and disappeared on the murky trail of the salt route.

In the dead of the night, he came out and disappeared on the murky trail of the salt route.

Sange Dorjee's Gompa in the Lap of Amadablam

In the times of forgotten history, once there lived a Lama known as Sange Dorjee. One day he decided to travel around the world away from his Gompa situated on northern base of Chhomolungma.

Since this great edifice stood guard over his Rong Phu Gompa, Sange Dorjee had no problem regarding the Gompa's protection, even when he was away.

Sange sat upright and meditated on the actual inner quality of Chhomolungma.

He visualized the goddess riding a tiger. She had two hands, and wore a dazzling crown of jewels.

There was a brilliant necklace around her neck and other precious ornaments graced her arms and wrists.

She seemed to be gracing the peaks of the mountains. She smiled and appeared as a protector of the people, mother goddess of the Earth. Not just for Sange but for everyone in the region.

The physical hardships of the region did not hinder Lama Sange. The high or low trails did not hamper his progress since he had divine powers to fly to his desired destinations.

Flying over the white, glistening mountain peaks and watching wonders that lay below him, Sange reached Pangboche.

He found place a sheer piece of beauty. The towering of the great Amadablam edifice enhanced the allure of the setting. The flatness of the ground and the gurgling of the foamy white waters of the Imja Khola below added a magical effect, the way an artist's brush does to a landscape.

The scenery was dotted with the intermittent bursts of flowering rhododendrons, and bhojpatra plants around Deujae.

The flocks of Danphe and Chilima were flying in and out of the bushes. Deujae, Tyangboche and Mingmo enjoying every bit of what they were facing. Large herds of *jharal* (mountain goat) dozed at the base of the mountain peaks.

Lothse, the tip of Chhomolungma and Kangtega sent a thrill of rapture though him.

Gazing at this wonderful scene and celebrating its awed magnificence, Dorjee remained speechless for sometime. He placed his foot on a stone and began to meditate.

On reaching Pangboche, he shaved off his long beard. The beard was blown away by the wind and spread all around Pangboche area.

Right there pine juniper trees sprung from the hair of his shaved beard. The trees encircled Pangboche like a garland of compassion and love.

The trees that sprung from the beard of Sange were considered sacred. At the same time Dablam became the favorite ornament to be hung around a Sherpa mother's neck.

Pumori became the daughter of the mountains, and Kangtega became the stirrup of the horse.

He visualized the goddess riding a tiger. She had two hands, and wore a dazzling crown of jewels.

And the people started venerating Sange Dorjee throughout the Khumbu region as an incarnated Rinpoche.

Snow Slide on Dorje's Salt

Many many years ago, a Sherpa named Lakpa Dorje lived in Beding village of Rolwaling. Lakpa earned his livelihood by bringing salt from Bhot and exchanging it with flour. But this year, early in the winter, he set out for Bhot along with Pashang Norbu.

As he had already been to the plains to exchange last year's collected herbs and medicinal items, *jimmu*, *nirmasi*, *himkhar* and *silajit*, for various types of foodstuff, Dorje was feeling confident and protected this winter. Though the season for salt-trading was almost over for the year, he had plenty of stock to survive.

For four months of a year, the Beding village would be enveloped under the cloak of snow. For this reason, Lakpa Dorje's family had to move down to a safer place known as Chhangmiga.

In Chhangmiga, like other migrated families, Dorje too had to make temporary arrangement for lodging. For not being in a position to arrange a good stock of foodstuff, even here there was every possibility for Beding people to die of hunger in the freezing winter. The life there was extremely harsh and deplorable.

To tell the truth, Beding village, surrounded by mountains on three sides and positioned on the edge of a raging brook, looked like an island without an ocean.

The dense lush green forest of pines, deodar, and cedar on the southern mountains had enhanced the glamour of this celestial valley. That's why, in spite of being far-flung and harsh, the villagers were emotionally attached to this place.

Dorje and Pashang Norbu set out with a flock of *zopkioks*. The jingling notes of the bells hanging around the zopkioks' neck engrossed them.

Soon they lost the sense of time and space. On the trail, there were no human inhabitants and there lurked the fear of thieves and dacoits over their heads.

However, this time they fell into the booby-trap of a ghost girl.

On the second night, they selected their usual camp in a huge cave before sunset. They did not have any idea to the number of rooms that cave contained in its various folds. Dorje started cooking. Pashang went out to collect dry twigs of cypress for firewood.

Suddenly Dorje heard a vicious sound, which gradually, kept moving closer to him. Though he felt a bit scared without his friend, he did not act cowardly. He had come across several thieves and looters during his previous business trips to Tibet.

As the sound came closer, Dorje learnt that it was a woman's voice. Soon a woman appeared and asked Dorje the reason of entering the cave without her permission.

She asked him to pay penalty for encroaching into her territory. The penalty was not in terms of food grains or salt, but in satisfying her lust for the night.

Unaware of Dorje's ploy, the woman guided
him into an antechamber.

As the penalty was being thrashed out, Norbu came with bunch of cypress firewood. Dorje accepted the woman's condition and secretly placed a tiny speck of cypress in his urinary track

Unaware of Dorje's ploy, the woman guided him into an antechamber. The room was well decorated and charming. Both lay on bed and soon engaged in the act. Yet because of that speck in the track of the male organ, she wriggled with pain, accepted her defeat even without getting her full satisfaction.

In reality, she was pretending to be the ghost girl of the cave. Dorje instructed her not to torture any traveler and trekker going to Bhot. He asked her to swear in the name of Lord Buddha.

The night passed. The dazzling sun rose out of the snow clad mountains. Dorje and Norbu started their onward journey. Having camped at various caves for three days, they reached the salt mine of Bhot before sunset.

Because of the snowfall, there was no salt merchant present for the bargain. Dorje and his friends loaded the salt onto their *zopkioks*, and spent the night there.

Soon it began to snow again. It was not possible to reach the village Chhangmiga directly.

Dorje and Norbu were happy of having cheated the merchants by not paying salt-money and tax. Jubilant, they decided to head for Nangpala. Though the passage of Nangpala was very long and tiring, it was easy to reach Namche Bazar

Nangpala was an easy but busy way through Khumbu towards Bhot. After five days' journey, Dorje and his friend Norbu reached the Khumbu valley

They had not known what happened outside
in the dead of the night.

through Nangpala. This is the place where Bhotekosi River meets Dhudkoshi River.

Below the pass in the lake of the mountains, Thami village slept quietly. The quivering flags above Thami monastery made their hair stand erect.

Thrilling notes of the monks engaged in evening prayers boomed in their mind. They recalled their own village and the monastery. Once again, the vision of their birthplace flashed before their eyes.

The village was silent and cold. The villagers clustered around the fireplace. Dorje and his friend took shelter in an old woman's house. On seeing Dorje and his friend, she fondly remembered her own son.

She was very young when her husband died. She would have married to settle for a normal life. But for her son's sake, she had not married.

Currently, her son had gone to bhot for kasturi business. Recalling her son, she let Dorje and his friend stay there for the night.

They exchanged salt for flour with the old woman. Norbu made a puddle of maize flour. Being tired from a long journey, they fell into a deep sleep.

As the morning Sun came out of the darkness, it became visible that it had snowed heavily last night. They had not known what happened outside in the dead of the night.

The salt had melted due to snow and zopkioks too had died.

This time Dorje did not have to pay tax and money for salt because the salt traders had already migrated to the plains. Dorje's plans to earn rich profit out of salt trading crashed. He wasn't much tortured for the loss of salt.

However, it was impossible to bear the pain resulting from the death of zopkioks, his entire lifetime's property.

Failing to concentrate, he sat for long time, watching the snowfall disconsolately.

The Ravishing of Angnima by a Yeti

Once the Sherpas inhabited regions known as Khumjang. In Khumjang, there lived a Sherpa named Sange Nawa. The people there had entrusted him with the responsibility of a protecting forests.

His son plied the trade route from Thami via Nangpa La to Tibet beyond the Himalayas. His daughter Angni, stayed home, and took the herd of yaks for grazing to the highland pastures.

One day as usual before the Dhumji festival, Angnima herded her cattle towards the alpine pastures.

The labor of climbing up and down made her exceedingly tired. She found a pile of dried branches of pine trees and sat down to rest.

Her herd grazed on the pastures all by itself while the warmth of the pine needless and the cool breeze softly caressed her and in a little while lulled her to sleep. Her eyes suddenly grew heavy and finally she fell into a deep slumber.

Angnima was a virgin Sherpa girl of twenty years. Due to shy nature, she did not have a male friend or a lover. However, sometimes she used to imagine what her future lover-husband might look like.

This is what she was wondering when on a warm, pleasant, but fatal afternoon she dozed off under the fragrant tree.

At this moment, a Yeti watched the yaks grazing from distant crags. He spotted Angnima blissfully asleep. He overlooked the yaks and turned his attention to the young innocent maiden looking stunningly beautiful in her sleep.

Instantly, lust lit up his eyes. He advanced, looking around in caution, walking with noiseless steps. Without delay, the Yeti reached the side of the girl sleeping the sleep of the one damned.

He took off Angima's *angki*, then *docha*, yet she did not wake up. Suddenly the Yeti threw himself on the girl and began the sexual assault.

The pressure and the resultant pain caused Angnima to wake up with searing pain. Dread surfaced in her eyes when she saw a strange creature defiling her.

Finally, an air-splitting scream came out of mouth. Unfortunately, no one except the crags and pasturelands and the dumb yak endlessly grazing could hear those helpless screams.

Angnima realized that rescue was impossible and panicked. The next moment, she became unconscious.

It was getting dark. Sange worried that his daughter had not yet returned with the yak herd. She had never been late like this, he said to himself. He felt very helpless. His son was also off on a business trip to Tibet and the darkness was slowly enveloping the hills. Sange did not know what to do.

He advanced, looking around in caution,
walking with noiseless steps.

Finally accompanied by a neighbor, he moved towards the hills and together they went up the slope. Soon they saw some yaks grazing on the slopes. Then they spotted the remaining herd. Having had their fill, the others lay huddled in a corner, munching. Angnima was nowhere to be seen.

They called out to her. Only the hills answered her name in mockery. The light in the sky was growing lesser and lesser when Sange spotted something crumpled beneath a pile of the rocks. Breathless, he rushed to the spot.

Yes, it was Angnima asleep there and Sange was happy.

"Angnima! Angnima" he called out. But she did not wake up. Feeling her pulse and forehead, he knew she was alive. Then Sange saw something that froze his heart in his chest.

Angnima was naked. The situation was grim. This meant his daughter had been sexually assaulted.

There was nothing he could do right now. Stumbling in the darkness, Sange and his friend carried Angnima back to the village.

As they reached the village, the news spread like wildfire. Everyone came to sympathize and kept pointing their accusing fingers towards the mountains where the dreaded Yeti lived.

A vigil was observed and it was only hours later that Angnima regained consciousness. She was unable to talk intelligibly. Only a string of jumbled sounds came from her throat.

There was nothing he could do right now. Stumbling
in the darkness, Sange and his friend carried
Angnima back to the village.

As the night deepened, she began to articulate her suffering more clearly. Slowly she came into her senses.

At this time, her father asked her questions. What really happened on that mountain slope that fatal afternoon? Then the tale of horror gradually spilled forth from Angnima's mouth in a soft quivering voice while the listeners sucked in their breath in disbelief and suppressed anger.

When Angnima's narrative reached the crucial moment where the Yeti crushed her tender body, she fainted once more. The night passed gradually until the morning arrived.

Next day she was fully conscious and even began eating. However, she was unable to utter a single word.

As the days passed, Angnima slowly lost her health, charm, and vitality and shrank into a pathetic mass of nerves.

Thus a month passed. One day Angnima opened her mouth to utter one unintelligible shriek but shut her mouth and then her eyes, never to speak or see again.

She fell into a deep sleep never to wake up again.

Tit for Tat

Once a Sahu of Besi Camp thought of visiting his friend's village. Carrying his train of *jyopkos*, the friend had gone to Bhot to bring salt and Sahu found himself alone with his friend's wife, Angfuti. She welcomed her husband's friend and entertained him by offering fried buff meat and local wine.

The night came. Intoxicated, both got entangled in sweet exchange of dialogues. Angfuti possessed two bodies then.

"Your belly has ballooned. Aren't you well or what?" Dharm Ratna asked.

"Oh, it's long since your friend locked it and went away to Bhot. Since that day this belly has been ballooning. He is not here. Now who is there to open this lock?" she replied.

Shrewd and much traveled, Dharm Ratna right away understood the whole point.

There was no one there except both of them. The night grew colder every minute and they kept on drinking more and more of the local beer boiling on the fiery hearth. The blaze of the local beer *chyang* continued to warm their bodies.

Then at last, Dharm Ratna decided to open the lock of his friend's wife.

Thinking that the balloon of her belly would subside, Angfuti too agreed. Having covered themselves under a warm quilt, they settled the deal.

Dharma Ratna opened Angfuti's lock. Now convinced that the ballooned belly would go down, she felt relieved. Then both moved to the bed and soon slipped into a dream.

The night passed. The bright seeds of the morning glory shot up. Uncertain of his friend's arrival, Dharm Ratna decided to leave. He did not wait for his arrival. Early in the dawn, he tumbled down towards the valley.

Carrying *jyopkos* of salt, Norbu returned home after some days. Angfuti was not expecting.

She casually told him the details of Dharm Ratna's arrival. She also narrated the story of opening up of the lock and the consequent improvement in her health.

Much experienced, Norbu wasn't as innocent as Angfuti. He understood each implication of Dharm Ratna's trick. He felt hurt within, though he didn't let Angfuti know his inner anger.

Time passed. One day he reached Dharm Ratna's house. The friend's wife, Shankhmaya was alone in the house because Dharm Ratna had gone to Lhasa for business.

Since the day her husband left, she was not in good health. She was suffering from the disease that women have to hide. As Dharm Ratna hadn't returned for months, she was quite upset. She was surprised to see Norbu at her door.

"Your belly has ballooned. Aren't you well or what?"
Dharm Ratna asked.

"Aren't you well or what?" on noticing his friend's wife's face, he asked.

"Since the day your friend left, I have been unhealthy. Would you please examine my state?" she politely asked.

"The Forest-God is very angry with you," Norbu whispered after a brief examination. "The God asks for a pot of wine and a fat cockerel."

Shankhmaya, the wife of Norbu's friend arranged all required things for the appeasement of the Forest-God. Both went across the neighboring hill range to pray to the Lord in the jungle.

They bathed a stone in local wine and added it to a pile of stone lying at the Lord's place. Then they sacrificed the young cockerel. She fried the meat while Norbu kept chanting mantras to appease the Lord.

Shankhmaya animatedly watched Norbu struggling to free her of pain. However, the Lord on no account seemed to come down to relieve Shankhmaya's pain. Both started taking meat and local beer.

"The disease can't be cured without putting up a lock, Norbu hollered in a strange shamanic language."

After a while, for the ailing Shankhmaya, Norbu became the Forest-God. Scared that it would block her urinary passage, she initially hesitated. Nevertheless, she was ready to do anything to cure herself. ...*Norbu then held her hand....and locked her!*

After that, it was all over. Even the Forest-God got appeased. Both came back home. Norbu too did not wait for his friend's arrival. He set out for his house.

"The Forest-God is very angry with you," Norbu whispered after a brief examination. "The God asks for a pot of wine and a fat cockerel."

Several months passed. Dharm Ratna returned from Lhasa. He was in high spirits as he had earned much gold and silver from the business trip.

Shankhmaya casually narrated the story of Norbu's arrival and his efforts to cure her malady. She also told him the fact of Norbu's locking her belly. She was of two bodies now.

Dharm Ratna grew quiet. He recalled his act of opening the lock that fateful night and now realized the meaning of Norbu's act of locking the belly of his own wife.

Yeti's Cave

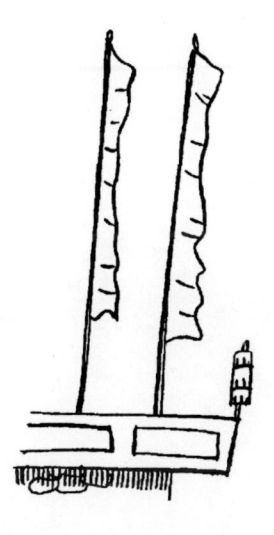

It is a tale of long ago. Angdorje Sherpa headed towards Chhiringma Himal's base in search of tubers of herbs. He roamed all day long and in the evening reached a glade where he found the tubers that he searched in plenty.

While he was collecting the tubers, the sun set down.

Angdorje did not have the heart to go back home all alone in the dark. He resolved to spend the night by the fireside in a cave.

Next morning as the sun rose, he came out. He was just looking around that he chanced to see a tiny child-like figure moving on the slope opposite him. The sun was dazzling. The flash made his eyesight blurred.

For a second he closed his eye to make sure what the figure looked like. As the day's speed increased, the shape, length and feature of the strange creature became more and more visible.

A hairy animal with forehead covered with hair, and dull pointed mouth made him feel nervous. There was no way to escape because he had to cross very steep and dangerous hills to reach home.

The creature was only a hundred yards father off. Then abruptly as it gained its complete larger-than-life-size, it stared moving towards Angdorje. When it became unbearable for him to face it anyfurther, he rushed backwards towards the cave where he had spent the night.

However, before he was only half way through, a flash of lighting slapped his eyes and he fell to the ground and became unconscious.

When Angdorje woke up, he found him in a different cave. It was a locked cell and there wasn't any visible way out. The granite wall of the cave emitted strange sparkling light. He noticed that he was himself lying in a warm fur mattress, seemingly made of yak's soft skin.

Due to hunger and fatigue, he was hardly able to move his limbs. The food lying around him was of curious type and he noticed a furry body softly caressing him. It didn't take Angdorje long to make out that that hairy creature was a woman because it possessed feminine appeal of his wife. Broken with hunger and fatigue, he ate the strange food reluctantly.

The food, though strange in appearance, was delicious to eat. Instead of water, there lay some liquid food in a leather bowl. He didn't find much difference between that liquid food and *Shykpa* with which he had grown up.

The moment Angdorje finished his meal, the hairy woman kissed him on the eyes and moved towards the gate of the cave muttering something strange. Then she kicked hard on the wall. The door of the cave opened.

She made a gesture with her hands and then moved out. The door shut by itself. After an hour, she came back carrying some more food and a quilt for the night. She placed the things in front of herself and grinned.

After an hour, she came back carrying some
more food and a quilt for the night. She placed
the things in front of herself and grinned.

Angdorje hadn't gone out but he knew it was night because he felt sleepy and his eyes burned. All night long, the hairy woman slept with him and made love to him. He didn't find any difference between his wife and that hairy creature. They played in bed until late in the night and then he fell asleep, unaware.

As he woke up, the hairy woman wasn't there and the place was locked. He recalled his home, his young wife, and other villagers. He was sure that that hairy woman wouldn't kill him because she had made him her lover. After sometime, the door of the cave opened. The same lovely hairy woman entered with fresh food. That day they ate together from the same plate.

By and by Angdorje started forgetting everything else. All he remembered was this woman. Even though his life wasn't completely secure, he started having strong feeling for her.

Thus the days passed. Everyday the hairy woman would go out after meals and he would recall his family members as usual. He would feel extremely bored in her absence. There wasn't anything to cook in case he felt hungry.

There wasn't any need of fire in the cave. She possessed leather and stone pots. He was lying in the fur quilt when the hairy woman entered. As usual, they played the game of love and went to sleep. Thus, the time passed and Angdorje became prisoner of the cave.

One day the hairy woman of the cave said something incomprehensible to him and then grinned. She made him sit on her lap, and caressing him pointed towards the door. Then she put on him a

He was astonished. He couldn't see anything but
Angdorje followed by a Yeti.

leather gown like garments to make him warm. She muttered something and then kicked hard on the wall. The door opened.

Holding his hand, she brought him out of the cave. Angdorje felt ecstatic. He was able to see the world after several months.

The sun was shining bright and the snow-capped mountains were dazzling. The cold wave of snowy winter made him shudder. They started to walk hand in hand lost in memory and he felt like escaping.

Even though it was freezing cold, Angdorje took off his *Docha* and asked her to put them on. At first, she refused but then she put them on for she was deep in love with him. They kept on walking on snow, frolicking.

Due to snow and water, *Docha* became heavy and wet. But she kept on walking even though she felt dizzy from heavy *Docha*. She didn't want to say anything that would hurt her lover.

The hairy woman had brought Angdorje out of the cave to transfer him to a new cave for some reason. However, while walking with her lover she forgot her plan and kept on walking with him enamored by his moves. She wasn't sure of the place she would reach.

Angdorje was moving towards his village and it was now at a short distance only. Engrossed in their amorous exchanges, they reached by the side of the village monastery.

That moment, Awatari was not there but Thawa was standing outside monastery. He was astonished. He couldn't see anything but Angdorje followed by a Yeti.

Yeti too was shocked to see another human being and a village. In her puzzle state of mind, she couldn't think of running away.

Thawa and other villagers imprisoned the Yeti in the monastery. Just then, Angdorje discovered that he had been with a yeti for so long.

Everyone praised him for being able to come back secure instead of being killed by a Yeti. His wife and five-year-old Angnima were also happy to welcome him back at home.

He had remained out of his house for more than a year. The villagers had gone out in search of him but had seen only the footprints of a Yeti.

In ecstasy, the villagers put a Khata on him and drank local beer wildly.

Next morning, they went back to the monastery. But Yeti wasn't there any more. Awatari was able to see her footprints only. The villagers were happy to have Angdorje back. They took it to be Angdorje's incarnation.

Nirala Series
A Series of Contemporary Writing

Ritual: The Magical Perspective
Efficacy an the Search for Inner Meaning
Luc Sala
ISBN 9-788182-500617 2014 Hard pp.832

The Mystery Over Lord Buddha's Roots
An Analysis of the Mystery of the Shakya Kingdom
Mitsuaki KOJIMA
ISBN 9-788182-500563 2014 Hard pp.165

Nine New York Poems: *A Prelude*
To A Blizzard In My Bones: New York Poems
Yuyutsu RD Sharma
ISBN 9-788182-500587 2014   Hard pp.64

Space Cake, Amsterdam
& Other Poems from Europe and America
Yuyutsu RD Sharma
ISBN 9-788182-500594 2014   Hard pp. 110

Pez / Fish
A Bilingual Edition
Mariela Dreyfus
Translated from the Spanish by **E.M. O'Connor**
ISBN 9-788182-500556 2014 Hard pp.64

TEN: The New Indian Poets
Selected and Edited by
Jayanta Mahapatra & Yuyutsu Sharma
ISBN 9-788182-500341 2012 pp.134 Hard

Dada Poetry
An Introduction
William Seaton
Foreword by **Timothy Shipe**
ISBN-9-788182-500358 2013 Hard pp.112

Libraries, Information Centers &
Information Professionalism in Nepal
Madhusudan Karki
ISBN 9-788182-500372 2012 Hard pp.348

Little Creek & Other Poems
David Austell
ISBN 9-788182-500549 2014 Paper pp.200

Student Politics & Democracy in Nepal
Meena Ojha
ISBN 9-788182-500259 2010 Hard pp.411

The Yeti
Spirit of Himalayan Forest Shamans
Larry G. Peters
ISBN 9-788182-500525   2014 Paper pp.128

Folk Tales of Sherpa and Yeti
Collected by Shiva Dhakal
Adapted by Yuyutsu RD Sharma
ISBN 81-8250-062-1 2014 Paper pp.125

The Gurkha Connection
A History of Gurkha Recruitment in the British Army
Purushottam Baskota
ISBN 81-85693-77-3 2014 Paper pp.221 Rs.

Annapurnas & Stains of Blood
Life, Travel &Writing on a page of Snow
Yuyutsu R D Sharma
ISBN 9-788182-500129 2010 Hard pp.200

Trance, Initiation & Psychotherapy in Nepalese Shamanism
Essays on Tamang and Tibetan Shamanism
Larry G.Peters
ISBN 9-788182-500532 2014 Paper pp.412

Tamang Shamans
An Ethnopsychiatric Study of Ecstasy and Healing in Nepal
Larry G. Peters
ISBN 9-788182-500099 2007 Paper pp.179

Ocean in a Drop
Yoga, Meditation and Life in the Himalayas
Swami Chandresh
ISBN 81-8250- 005-2 2006 Hard pp.348

Maoists in the Land of Buddha
An Analytical Study of the Maoist Insurgency in Nepal
Prakash A. Raj
ISBN 81-8250-2004 Hard pp.210

Rana Rule in Nepal
Shaphalya Amatya
ISBN 81-85693-67-6 2004 Hard pp.408

The Dhimals: Miraculous Migrants of Himal
An Anthropological Study of a Nepalese Ethnic Group
Rishikeshab Raj Regmi
ISBN 9-788182-500099 2014 Paper pp.269

The Gurungs: Thunder of Himal
A Cross-Cultural Study of a Nepalese Ethnic Group
Murari P. Regmi
ISBN 81-85693-49-8 2002 Paper pp.238

The Gurkhas
A History of the Recruitment in the British Indian Army
Kamal Raj Singh Rathaur
ISBN 81-85693-85-4 2000 Paper pp.128

Landlessness and Migration in Nepal
Nanda R. Shrestha
ISBN 81-85693-87-0 2001 Hard pp.309

Tourism in Nepal
Marketing Challenges
Hari Prasad Shrestha
ISBN 81-85693-69-2 2000 Hard pp.399

Ethnic Conflict in Bhutan
Political and Economic Dimensions
Mathew Joseph C.
ISBN 81-85693-68-4 1999 Hard pp.251

Recent Nepal
An Analysis of Recent Democratic Upsurge and its Aftermath
Laksman Bhadur K.C.
ISBN 81-85693-24-2 1993 Hard pp.242

Mountain Dimensions
An Altitude Geographic Analysis
of Environment and Development of the Himalayas
Ram Kumar Pandey
ISBN 81-85693-43-9 1999 pp.260 Hard

Wildlife in Nepal
Rishikesh Shaha & Richard M. Mitchell
With Color Plates by Nanda Shumsher J.B. Rana
ISBN 81-85693-31-5 2001 Paper pp.142

Nepal: Missing Elements in the Development Thinking
Gunanidhi Sharma
ISBN 81-85693-66-8 2000 Hard pp.282

Making of Modern Nepal
A Study of History, Art and Culture of the Principalities of Western Nepal
Ram Niwas Pandey
ISBN 81-85693-37-4 1997 Hard pp.816

Politics and Development in Nepal:
Some Issues
Narayan Khadka
ISBN 81-85693-21-8 1994 Hard pp.477

Hindu-Buddhist Festival of Nepal
Hemant Kumar Jha
ISBN 81-85693-40-4 1996 Hard pp.117

Art and Culture of Nepal
An Attempt towards Preservation
Saphalya Amatya
ISBN 81-85693-63-3 1999 Hard pp.282

Popular Deities, Emblems and Images of Nepal
Dhruba Krishna Deep
ISBN 81-85693-39-0 2003 Paper pp.180

Vishwarupa Mandir
A Study of Changu Narayan, Nepal's most Ancient Temple
Jeff Lidke
ISBN 81-85693-59-3 2000 Hard pp.213 Rs. 1495

Making of Modern Nepal
A Study of History, Art and Culture of the Principalities of Western Nepal
Ram Niwas Pandey
ISBN 81-85693-37-4 1997 Hard pp.816

Politics and Development in Nepal:
Some Issues
Narayan Khadka
ISBN 81-85693-21-8 1994 Hard pp.477

Indo-Nepal Trade Relations
A Historical Analysis of Nepal's Trade with the British India
Shri Ram Upadhyaya
ISBN 81-85693-20-X 1992 pp.287

Secrets of Shangri-La
An Inquiry into the Lore, Legend and Culture of Nepal
Nagendra Sharma
ISBN 81-85693-18-8   1992   pp.292

The Taming of Tibet
*A Historical Account of Compromise and Confrontation
in Nepal-Tibet Relations (1900-1930)*
Tirtha Prasad Mishra
ISBN 81-85693-16-1 1991 pp.324

Glimpses of Tourism, Airlines and Management in Nepal
B.R. Singh
ISBN 81-85693-15-3   1991   pp.128

Sales Promotion in Nepal
Policies and Practices
Parashar Prasad Koirala
ISBN 81-85693-14-5 1991 pp.196

Hindu-Buddhist Festival of Nepal
Hemant Kumar Jha
ISBN 81-85693-40-4   1996   Hard   pp.117

Transit of Land Locked Countries and Nepal
Gajendra Mani Pradhan
ISBN 81-85693-08-0   1990   pp.240

Fundamentals of Library and Information Science
A Nepalese Response •
Madhusudan Sharma Subedi
ISBN 81-85693-07-4 1990 pp.229

Folk Culture of Nepal
An Analytical Study
Ram Dayal Rakesh
ISBN 81-85693-06-4   1990 Hard   pp.129

A Macro-economic Study of the Nepalese Plan Performance
Gunanidhi Sharma
ISBN 81-85693-06-4   1989   pp.129

Sources of Inflation in Asia
Theory and Evidences
Raghab D. Pant
ISBN 81-85693-03-X   1988   Hard pp.118

New Directions in Nepal- India Relations
Rishikesh Shaha
ISBN 81-85693-53-6   1995   Paper pp.59

IN NEPALI LANGUAGE

Panaharu Khalichan : Kavitaka Dui Dashak (Poems)
Yuyustu R.D. Sharma
ISBN 81-8250-004-4   2008   Paper pp. 102

Pashushala   (Animal Farm) (A Novel)
Georege Orwell
Translated from the English by Bijuli Prasad Kayast
ISBN 81-8250-000-1   2004   Paper pp.96

Nepalko Prajatantrik Andolan Ko Itihas
Surya Mani Adhikary
ISBN 81-85693-54-4   1998   Paper pp.468

Geetajanjali (Nepali)
Rabindra Nath Tagore
Translated from the Bengali by **Ramesh Bhatta & Pashupati Neopane**
ISBN 81-85693-83-8   2000   Paper pp.125

Sarpahoru Geet Sundainan
Pomes by Shailendra Sakar
ISBN 81-85693-97-8   1991   Hard pp.108

Nirala Series
A Series of Contemporary Literature

Annapurna Poems
Yuyutsu R D Sharma
ISBN 81-8250-013-5 2008 Hard pp.150

After Tagore
Poems Inspired by **Rabindranath Tagore**
David Ray
ISBN 81-8250-007-9 2008 Hard pp. 128

Kathmandu
Poems Selected and New (An English/Nepali Bilingual Edition)
Cathal O Searcaigh
Translated from the Gaelic by **Seamus Heaney,**
John Montague and others
Translated into the Nepali by *Yuyutsu R.D. Sharma*
ISBN 81-8250-006-0 2006 Hard pp. 105

The Lake Fewa & a Horse
Poems New
Yuyutsu R.D. Sharma
ISBN 81-8250-015-X 2008 Paper pp. 108

Muna Madan
A Play in the Jhyaure Folk Tradition
Laxmi P. Devkota
Translated from the Nepali by **Anand P. Shrestha**
ISBN 81-8250-014-1 2007 pp.65

Fever (Short Stories)
Sita Pandey
Translated from the Nepali
ISBN 81-85693-93-5 2001 Paper pp.96

Says Meera
An Anthology of Devotional Songs of Meera, India's Greatest Woman Poet
Translated from the Hindi by **Vijay Munshi**
ISBN 81-85693-96-X 2001 Paper pp.76

Some Female Yeti & other Poems
Yuyutsu R.D.
ISBN 81-8250-010-9 2008 pp.68

In the City of Partridges (Poems)
Jagdish Chatturvedi
ISBN 81-85693-99-4 2004 Paper pp.90

Roaring Recitals: Five Nepali Poets
Gopal Prasad Rimal, Bhupi Sherchan, Shailendra & Others
Translated from the Nepali by
Yuyutsu R.D. Sharma
ISBN 81-85693-95-1 1999 Hard pp.99

Summer Rain
Three Decades of Poetry
K. Satchidanandan
ISBN 81-85693-90-0 1995 Paper pp.188

Sheet of Snow
An Anthology of Stories from the Himalayas
Translated from the Nepali by **Nagendra Sharma**
ISBN 81-85693-61-7 1997 paper pp.125

Dispossessed Nests: The 1984 Poems
Jayanta Mahapatra
ISBN 81-85693-74-9 1986 pp.69 Paper

To the Battlefield on an Elephant
Columns of Fire
Tara Nath Sharma
ISBN 81-85693-44-7 1999 pp.164 paper

The Change
A Novel based on the 1990 Democratic Upsurge in Nepal
Rishikeshab Raj Regmi
ISBN 81-85693-62-5 2001 pp.125

Blackout (A Novel) Tara Nath Sharma
Translated from the Nepali by **Larry Hartsell**
ISBN 81-85693-82-X 1990 pp.122

Elysium in the Halls of Hell
Poems about India **David Ray**
ISBN 81-85693-84-6 1991 pp.160

A Prayer in Daylight (Poems)
Yuyutsu R.D.
ISBN 81-85693-72-2 1984 paper pp.68

Hunger of Our Huddled Huts & Other Poems
Yuyutsu R.D.
ISBN 81-85693-80-3 2007 pp.65

Dying in Rajasthan (Short Stories)
Ramanand Rathi
ISBN 81-85693-71-4 1985 pp.62

The Black Sun (A Novel)
Bharat Jungam
ISBN 81-85693-84-6 1985 pp.78